The RED SOX

and the World Series

by Morgan Clendaniel

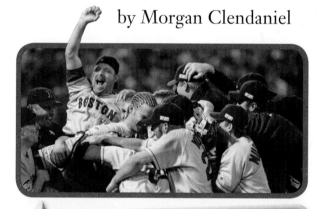

Strategy Focus

As you read, **evaluate** the facts and opinions about this famous baseball team.

HOUGHTON MIFFLIN   BOSTON

Key Vocabulary

consecutive one after the other

fielding picking up a baseball and throwing it to the right player

first baseman a baseball player who guards the area near first base

honor to show special respect for

modest not proud or boastful

shortstop a baseball player who guards the area between second and third base

sportmanship acting fairly about winning and losing

Word Teaser

Which baseball player never takes long pauses?

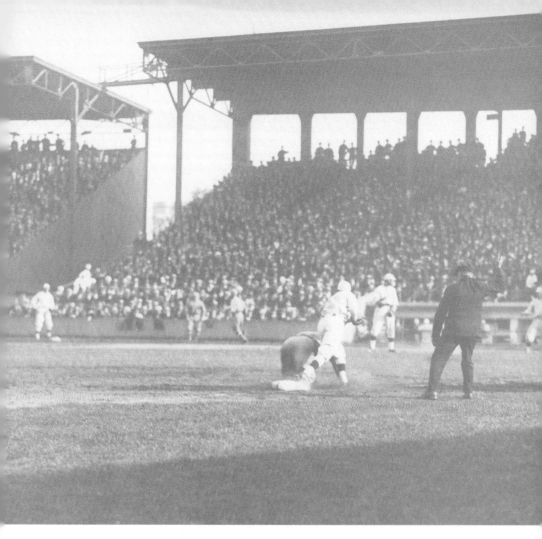

Fenway Park, Boston, Massachusetts

The Boston Red Sox are one of the oldest baseball teams in America. Fans in Boston love to watch the Red Sox play. But the fans had been unhappy for many years. Their team had not won a World Series since 1918.

Over the years, Red Sox players won many games. The fans still honor these great players. But the team never became World Champions.

In 2004, the Red Sox got a new pitcher named Curt Schilling. He was one of the best pitchers in all of baseball. He promised he would try to help the Red Sox win the World Series.

The Red Sox started the season by winning many games. They were in first place, but they were modest. They didn't think they were better than other teams.

Then the Red Sox started losing. Many of their players were hurt. The shortstop couldn't play. He was one of the most important players, but he had to stay out of the game.

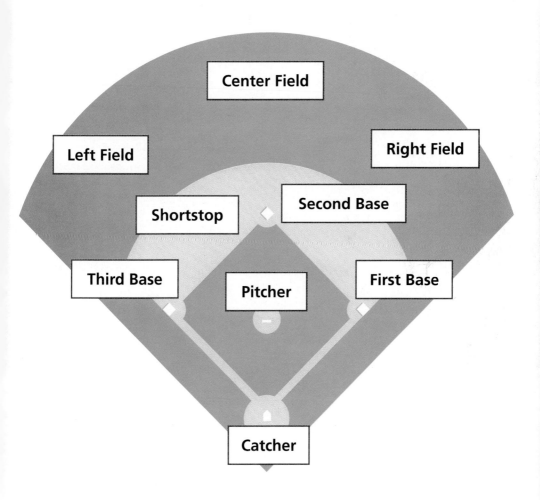

The Red Sox knew that they were not doing a good job fielding the balls the other team hit. So they got new players who were better at picking up the ball.

The new players made a difference. The Red Sox started winning many games in a row. They won ten consecutive games in August of 2004.

Before they could play in the World Series, the Red Sox had to beat the New York Yankees in another series of games called playoff games. The team that won four out of seven games would play in the World Series.

The Yankees had won 26 World Series since 1918. The Red Sox hadn't won any. The Yankees won the first three playoff games. Things looked very bad for the Red Sox.

The fans in Boston couldn't believe it. Would the Red Sox lose as they had so many times before?

The Red Sox won the fourth and fifth playoff games. In the sixth game, Curt Schilling played even though his ankle was bleeding. He pitched a great game and the Red Sox won. He was a hero who showed courage and good sportsmanship.

The Red Sox won the seventh game the next night. Now the Red Sox had the chance to go to the World Series and win again!

In the World Series, the Red Sox played the St. Louis Cardinals. The Red Sox won the first three games easily. They only needed to win one more game to win the World Series.

At the end of the fourth game, the Red Sox were winning. The Red Sox fans held their breath. The Cardinals' last batter hit the ball to the Red Sox pitcher. The pitcher threw it to the first baseman. The batter was OUT! The game was over.

The unbelievable had happened. The Red Sox had won the World Series! Their loyal fans cheered and cried. After 86 long years, their team had finally become World Champions!

Putting Words to Work

1. Why is good **fielding** important in baseball?

2. Complete this sentence: When I play a game, I show good **sportsmanship** by _____.

3. Tell one fact and one opinion about the 2004 World Series. Use the word **consecutive** in your fact.

4. Would you be **modest** after winning a game? Why or why not?

5. What person would you like to **honor**? Why?

6. **PARTNER ACTIVITY:** Think of a word you learned in the book. Explain its meaning to your partner and give an example.

Answer to Word Teaser
the **shortstop**